To Amadi and Elijawon
and all God's children,
I pray that you see yourself
as God sees you.
—Sara

To my mom and dad,
who showed me that
I came from greatness.
—Ken

YOU COME FROM

WATERBROOK

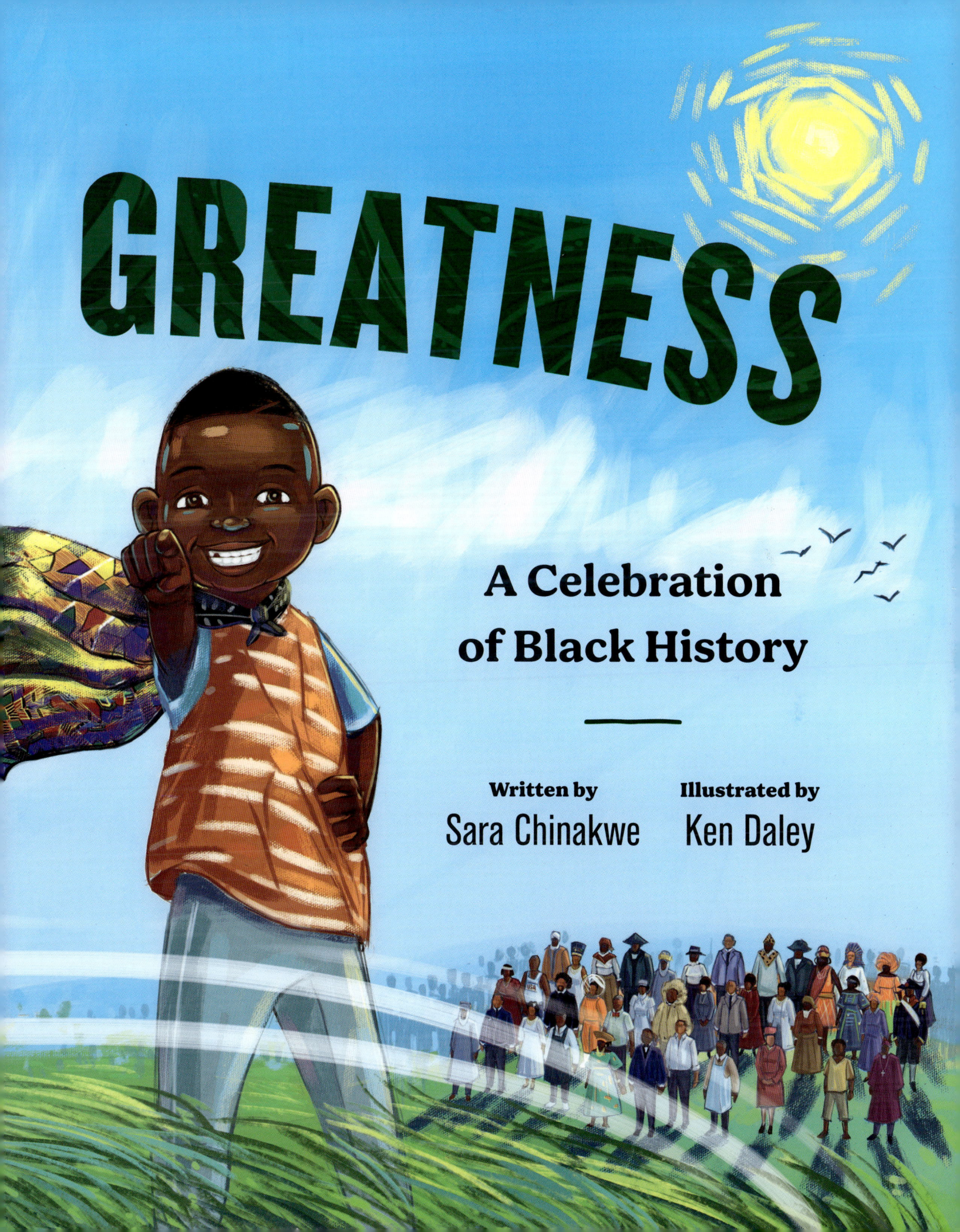

GREATNESS

A Celebration of Black History

Written by
Sara Chinakwe

Illustrated by
Ken Daley

You came bustling into the world, a mighty bundle of energy, ready to do great things.

Sojourner Truth, Henry "Box" Brown, Ida B. Wells-Barnett, Benjamin Banneker, Nefertiti, Jesse Owens, Sundiata Keita, Margaret Ekpo

And no wonder—you stand on the shoulders of those who came before, and you, too, were

BORN TO SHINE.

You come from laughter and love.
From a big family—by way of the bayou—who ate crawdads at the crab boil after Sunday service.

From a mother who's as warm as a brassy African sunset
and a father whose emboldened strength lies
just beneath his tender heart.
And you?

You embody a spirit that soars with delight over
new possibilities. You can go anywhere.
YOU CAN BE ANYTHING.

You come from people who spoke with voices as mighty as a lion's roar. You come from change makers and status shakers, people ready to rally in unity to ensure your future. Like them, you are a light that will spark the next generation.

Martin Luther King Jr., Rosa Parks, Wangari Muta Maathai, John Lewis

Don't be afraid to lift up your voice.
SPEAK PEACE AND SEEK JUSTICE!

You are descended from dreamers—designers, inventors, and engineers. If you listen closely, you can hear the clinkety-clank of their work. You come from dedication and determination.

Sarah Boone, Ellie Mannette, Garrett Morgan

Now pick up your tools, child,
and be a willing worker.
You are just the right person with
just the right ideas. Use the talent God
has given you to make a better world.

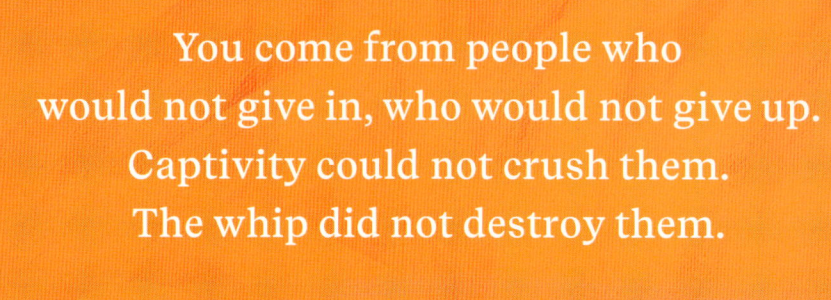

You come from people who
would not give in, who would not give up.
Captivity could not crush them.
The whip did not destroy them.

In songs of lament,
they poured out their pain,
then soared up again
with hopeful refrain.

Frederick Douglass, Harriet Tubman, Toussaint L'Ouverture

You come from strong backs
and stronger spirits.
Never forget that.
You have a proud heritage.
WALK TALL.

You come from great African tribes, who celebrated with ancient masquerades long into the night as the swish, swish, swish of their grass skirts moved to the boom, boom, boom of the drums.

You come from the islands, with the rhythm of reggae and calypso on the coast.

Miriam Makeba, Mahalia Jackson, Ma Rainey, B. B. King

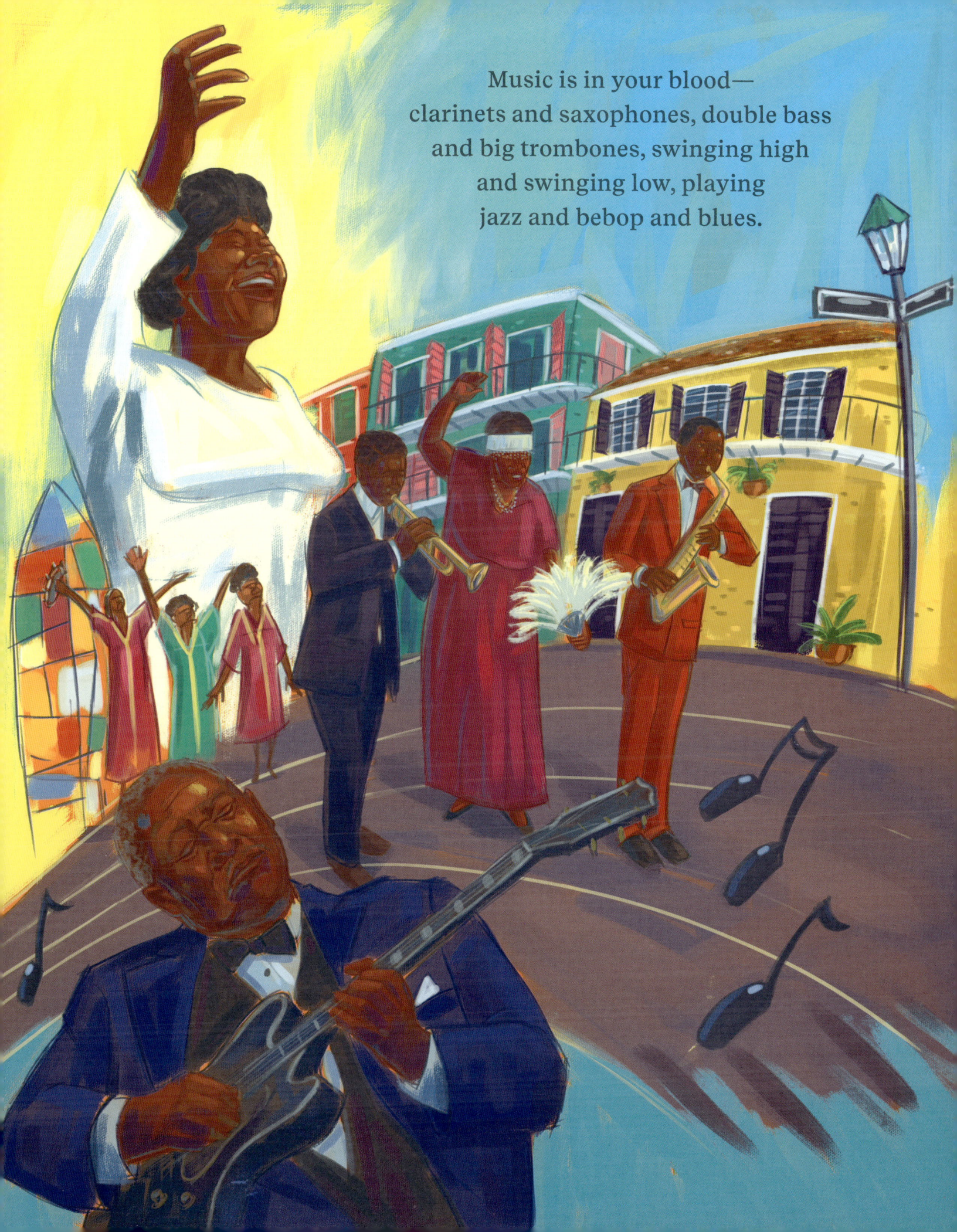

Music is in your blood—
clarinets and saxophones, double bass
and big trombones, swinging high
and swinging low, playing
jazz and bebop and blues.

And here you are, with your drumming and your humming and all your joyful noise.

With your rapping. With your shimmy and your shake.

SING ON. DANCE ON.

MOVE TO THE BEAT GOD GIVES YOU.

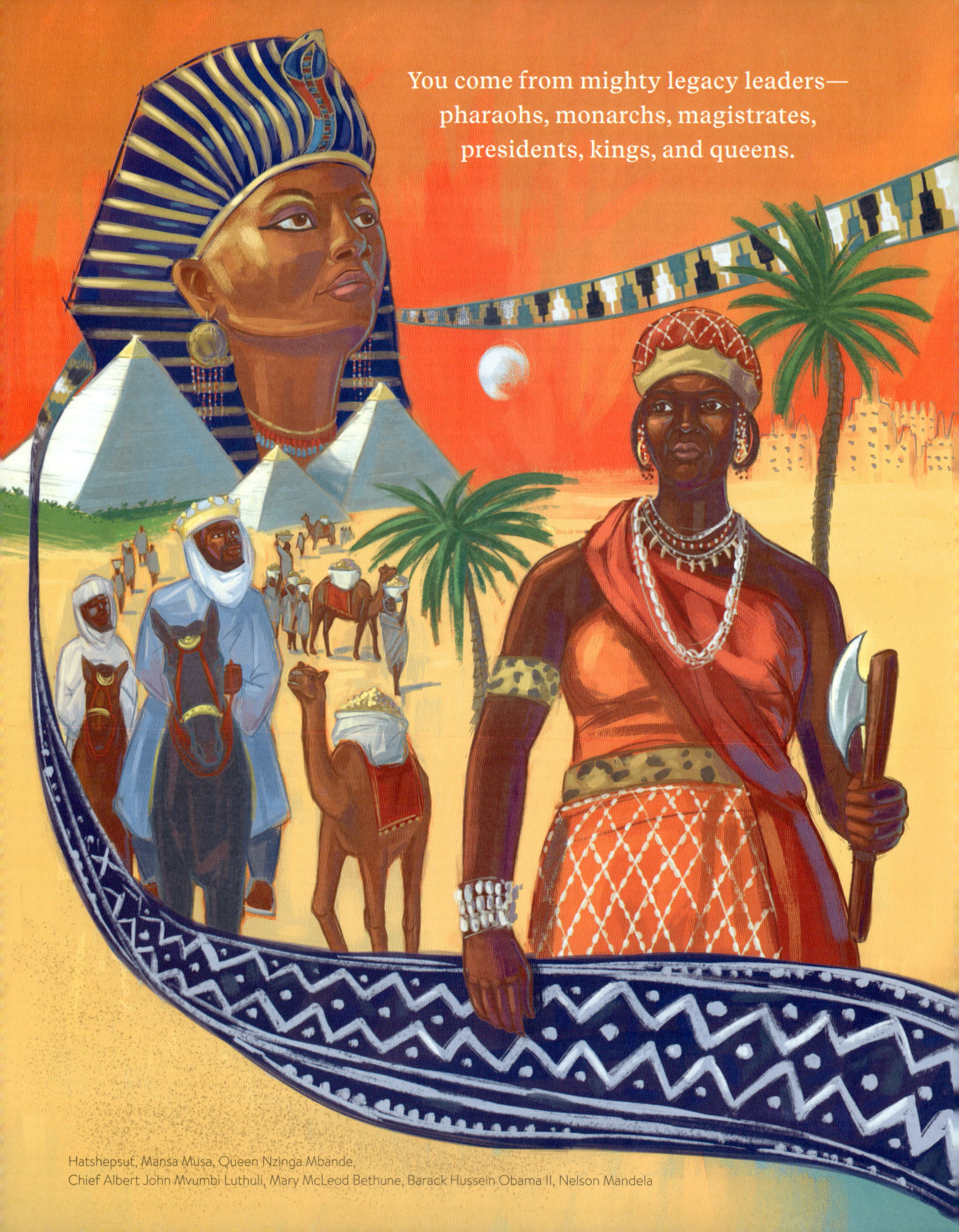

You come from mighty legacy leaders—
pharaohs, monarchs, magistrates,
presidents, kings, and queens.

Hatshepsut, Mansa Musa, Queen Nzinga Mbande,
Chief Albert John Mvumbi Luthuli, Mary McLeod Bethune, Barack Hussein Obama II, Nelson Mandela

HOPE

And if one day God raises you and seats you on a throne, I know you'll serve with grace and truth and **MAKE HIS GLORY KNOWN.**

You come from doctors and scientists and preachers—men and women who cared for bodies and souls. They bandaged the wounded, spoke truth in love, and served others first.

My child, follow their lead and let your unending love for others radiate like the ripples in a pond.

Desmond Tutu, Rebecca Lee Crumpler, Jane Cooke Wright

Feed the hungry, help the sick, clothe the needy,
and forgive as you've been forgiven.
Then you, too, can bring healing to this weary world.

You come from astronomers and mathematicians who mapped the paths of planets, navigated oceans and deserts, and calculated time and tides.

Their complex equations sent ships across oceans and kept caravans on course. They launched astronauts into space.

Mae Jemison, Matthew Henson, Euphemia Lofton Haynes

And then?
They brought them safely home again.

AND YOU?

You might use a telescope
to study the stars.
Or you may choose to fly—
far up high—above the earth.

Whatever you decide, work with diligence and soar with confidence because
GOD CREATED YOU TO SHINE
wherever you go in the universe.

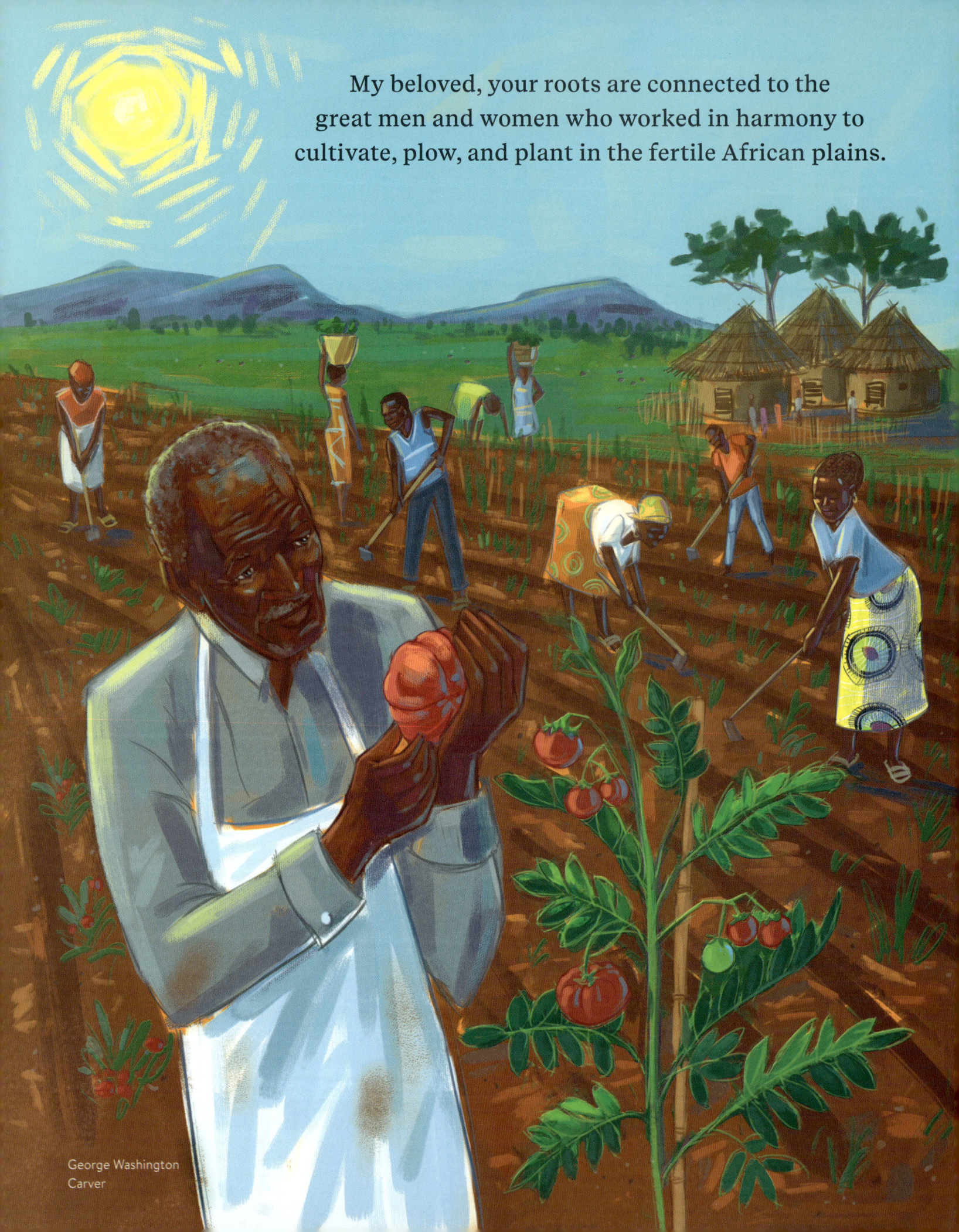

My beloved, your roots are connected to the great men and women who worked in harmony to cultivate, plow, and plant in the fertile African plains.

George Washington Carver

So farm the land that
God has laid before you.
Dig down into the dirt.
Plant and water and wait.

Sow the seeds and pull the weeds,
trusting that one day you will
ENJOY WHAT YOU GROW.

You come from wise poets, storytellers, and ancient desert dwellers, who were philosophers, prophets, and priests.

They shared their knowledge with generation after generation, sparking new possibilities and fanning the flames of change across time. Continue in their footsteps.

Maya Angelou, Jupiter Hammon, Anton Wilhelm Amo

KEEP THE FIRE BURNING,

my child. Live out your story, and tell the people you meet along the way about the good God who guides your life.

Because you see, my child, you come from God—
the Father, the Son, and the Holy Spirit.
The Creator, the Savior, the Guide.

He made you exactly the way you're supposed
to be—just the right texture, just the right hue.
He created *you*!

From your head to your toes and everything in between,

YOU ARE GREATNESS.

20 GREAT PEOPLE

MARTIN LUTHER KING JR. • 1929–1968
Bold Civil Rights Activist and Preacher

Martin Luther King Jr. was an African American Baptist preacher, Nobel Peace Prize recipient, and visible face of the civil rights movement. Dr. King fought injustice through the power of words and nonviolent protests, and his legacy can be seen throughout American history.

JOHN LEWIS • 1940–2020
Fearless Civil Rights Activist and US Politician

John Lewis was a widely respected African American civil rights activist and member of the House of Representatives. Considered one of the "Big Six" leaders of the civil rights movement, Lewis was involved in many peaceful protests including the March on Washington and the voting rights march from Selma to Montgomery, Alabama, which led to the passage of the 1965 Voting Rights Act.

WANGARI MUTA MAATHAI • 1940–2011
Esteemed Nobel Peace Prize Recipient

Wangari Muta Maathai spent her life serving others. As a Kenyan activist, she advocated for human rights, environmental sustainability, and AIDS prevention and was elected as a member of Kenya's National Assembly. Maathai was the first African woman to receive the Nobel Peace Prize, awarded for her conservation work.

SARAH BOONE • 1832–1904
Persistent Inventor and US Patent Recipient

Although Sarah Boone was born into slavery, once free, she started work as a dressmaker and envisioned a new way to iron clothes. After designing an improved ironing board, she became one of the first African American women to receive a US patent.

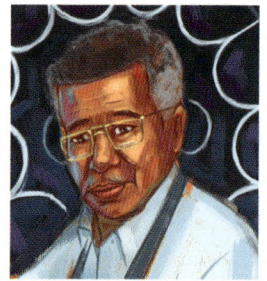

ELLIOTT "ELLIE" MANNETTE • 1927–2018
Innovative Steel Drum Maker

Born in Trinidad, Elliott "Ellie" Mannette is known as "the Father of the Modern Steel Drum." He redesigned the steel pan, originally crafted by enslaved Africans, and transformed old oil drums into the instruments we hear today. His reputation as a tuner and pannist grew until he became an ambassador for the steel pan (or steel drum), and his influence can now be heard in bands all over the world.

WHO CAME BEFORE YOU

TOUSSAINT L'OUVERTURE • 1743–1803
Brave Military Leader

During the French Revolution, Toussaint L'Ouverture was a prominent leader who fought to end slavery in Saint-Domingue (modern-day Haiti). Born enslaved, L'Ouverture secured his freedom, then took part in a successful slave rebellion. He became a renowned military commander, and eventually governed Saint-Domingue.

HARRIET TUBMAN • 1820–1913
Heroic Freedom Fighter

Harriet Tubman was an American hero who fought tirelessly for her people. She guided enslaved African Americans to freedom via a system of secret routes called the Underground Railroad. Later, she worked as a nurse, scout, and spy during the Civil War, becoming the first African American woman to serve in the military.

MAHALIA JACKSON • 1911–1972
Influential American Gospel Singer

Born in poverty in New Orleans, Mahalia Jackson found her calling as a gospel singer in a church near her home. She delivered God's Word through music and used her voice as a civil rights activist both in Montgomery, Alabama, following the successful bus boycott, and at the March on Washington, where she sang before Dr. King's famous "I Have a Dream" speech.

MIRIAM MAKEBA • 1932–2008
Passionate Humanitarian and Entertainer

Miriam Makeba, nicknamed "Mama Africa," was a South African singer whose music shed light on apartheid (a form of segregation) in South Africa. Her legacy also includes her dedication to humanitarian work and her service as a United Nations Goodwill Ambassador.

BARACK HUSSEIN OBAMA II • 1961–
Groundbreaking Forty-Fourth President of the United States

During his time at Harvard Law School, Barack Hussein Obama II garnered attention as the first African American president of the *Harvard Law Review*. He moved to Chicago and was elected to the Illinois senate, then to the US Senate. In 2009, Obama became the first African American to hold the office of president of the United States of America.

NELSON MANDELA • 1918–2013
Resilient African Leader

Born with the name Rolihlahla Mandela, Nelson Mandela fought for the fair treatment of his people, which led to him being imprisoned for twenty-seven years. At age seventy-five, he became the first African of color to be elected president of South Africa.

QUEEN NZINGA MBANDE • 1581–1663
Fierce Queen of Ndongo and Matamba

In the seventeenth century, Queen Nzinga Mbande ruled Ndongo and Matamba (modern-day northern Angola). She was well known for her visionary leadership, which helped ward off invasion by the Portuguese, protecting her people from enslavement.

MARY MCLEOD BETHUNE • 1875–1955
Instrumental Leader for Education and Equality

Mary McLeod Bethune's passion for education, race, and gender equality propelled her to found a school that would become Bethune-Cookman University in Daytona Beach, Florida. Through her leadership in President Franklin D. Roosevelt's informal "Black Cabinet," Bethune paved the way for the US civil rights movement.

CHIEF ALBERT JOHN MVUMBI LUTHULI • 1898–1967
Courageous Activist

As a teacher, a religious leader, and the president of the African National Congress, Chief Albert John Mvumbi Luthuli advocated for an end to the unjust treatment of Black South Africans. He was known for his nonviolent struggle against racial discrimination and became the first African to be awarded the Nobel Peace Prize.

REBECCA LEE CRUMPLER • 1831–1895
Celebrated American Doctor

As a young girl, Rebecca Lee Crumpler was inspired by her aunt who cared for her sick neighbors. Despite common prejudices of the day, she was the first African American woman to become a doctor in the US and one of the first African American doctors to publish a medical book.

DESMOND TUTU • 1931–2021
Prominent Religious Leader

Desmond Tutu became the first Black South African to be appointed dean of St. Mary's Cathedral and the first African of color to hold position as bishop of Johannesburg. In 1984, he was awarded the Nobel Peace Prize for his work in opposition to apartheid in South Africa.

MATTHEW HENSON • 1866–1955
Extraordinary American Explorer

Matthew Henson was an African American explorer and the first man to reach the North Pole. Henson published a memoir of his adventure in *A Negro Explorer at the North Pole*. Later in life, he was invited to the White House as a guest under Presidents Truman and Eisenhower and awarded the Peary Polar Expedition Medal.

EUPHEMIA LOFTON HAYNES • 1890–1980
Brilliant Educator

Euphemia Lofton Haynes was the first African American woman to receive a PhD in mathematics. Haynes's long-standing love for education made her an influential leader in the African American school system. She trained teachers, denounced segregation in schools, and became the president of the District of Columbia Board of Education.

GEORGE WASHINGTON CARVER • 1864–1943
Accomplished Agricultural Scientist

George Washington Carver developed a crop rotation technique that used legumes to restore nutrients to the soil and ultimately increase crop yields. He also discovered new ways to use peanuts and sweet potatoes, creating hundreds of products including paints, soaps, cosmetics, and medicines.

ANTON WILHELM AMO • 1703–1759
Renowned Philosopher

Anton Wilhelm Amo was a notable Black philosopher in the eighteenth century. Born in present-day Ghana, he was the first African to study at a European university. His first academic work argued against the enslavement of Black people in Europe at a time when it was very dangerous to do so.

DISCOVER MORE STORIES OF GREAT PEOPLE

The ABCs of Black History by Rio Cortez

Black Heroes: 51 Inspiring People from Ancient Africa to Modern-Day U.S.A. by Arlisha Norwood

Brave. Black. First.: 50+ African Women Who Changed the World by Cheryl Willis Hudson

Little Leaders: Bold Women in Black History by Vashti Harrison

Little Legends: Exceptional Men in Black History by Vashti Harrison

Timelines from Black History: Leaders, Legends, Legacies by DK

You Come from Greatness

Text copyright © 2023
by Sara Chinakwe
Cover art and interior illustrations
copyright © 2023 by Ken Daley

All rights reserved.

Published in the United States by WaterBrook, an imprint of Random House, a division of Penguin Random House LLC.

WaterBrook® and its deer colophon are registered trademarks of Penguin Random House LLC.

ISBN 978-0-593-57828-5
EBOOK ISBN 978-0-593-57829-2

The Library of Congress catalog record is available at https://lccn.loc.gov/2021055321.

Printed in China

waterbrookmultnomah.com

10 9 8 7 6 5 4 3

First Edition

Cover design by Ashley Tucker
Book design by Sonia Persad and Ashley Tucker

Special Sales Most WaterBrook books are available at special quantity discounts when purchased in bulk by corporations, organizations, and special-interest groups. Custom imprinting or excerpting can also be done to fit special needs. For information, please email specialmarketscms@penguinrandomhouse.com.